THE INVISIBLE KINGDOM

Rob Ryan

Crocodile Books, USA

An imprint of Interlink Publishing Group, Inc.

www.interlinkbooks.com

IN THE LIVING ROOM IN OUR OLD HOUSE, sitting on the mantelpiece and on the wall all around it, was a collection of photographs of our family.

There were pictures of my brothers, my sister, and me taken when we were babies and very small children. There were pictures of Mum and Dad taken before we were born—they looked so young and happy, smiling together for the camera.

There were pictures of uncles and aunts and grandparents too. Pictures of people that we had known and pictures of people who were already dead before we were even born. Everything we knew about them was from listening to the stories told in this very room, sitting around the fire on cozy Sunday afternoons all winter long.

Even then the stories of some of their lives were beginning to fade, and now I hardly remember any of them at all.

Sooner or later nobody alive on this planet will know anything about any of the people in all those photographs, and that includes me.

But the story in this book isn't about a family that will one day be forgotten; in fact, rather the opposite.

THE FAMILY IN THIS STORY could tell you all about every single member of it who had ever lived, because this was a royal family. A dynasty of kings and queens who had reigned over their country for more than a thousand years.

But it was not only the family themselves who knew all the legends of their long-dead relations, so too did every woman and man in the land.

It was the law that every child should be taught about the lives of every monarch who had ever reigned. Every boy and girl could tell you about the terrible queen who killed her brother and the frightful king who did away with

his sister. There were bad kings who enslaved whole nations and good kings who set all the slaves free. There was a sweet and gentle queen who reigned until she was nearly one hundred years old; she was so loved by her people that when she died every eye in the kingdom wept at least one tear.

To understand the long story of the country, you just needed to look at the lives of the kings and queens and how the crown had passed from one head to another.

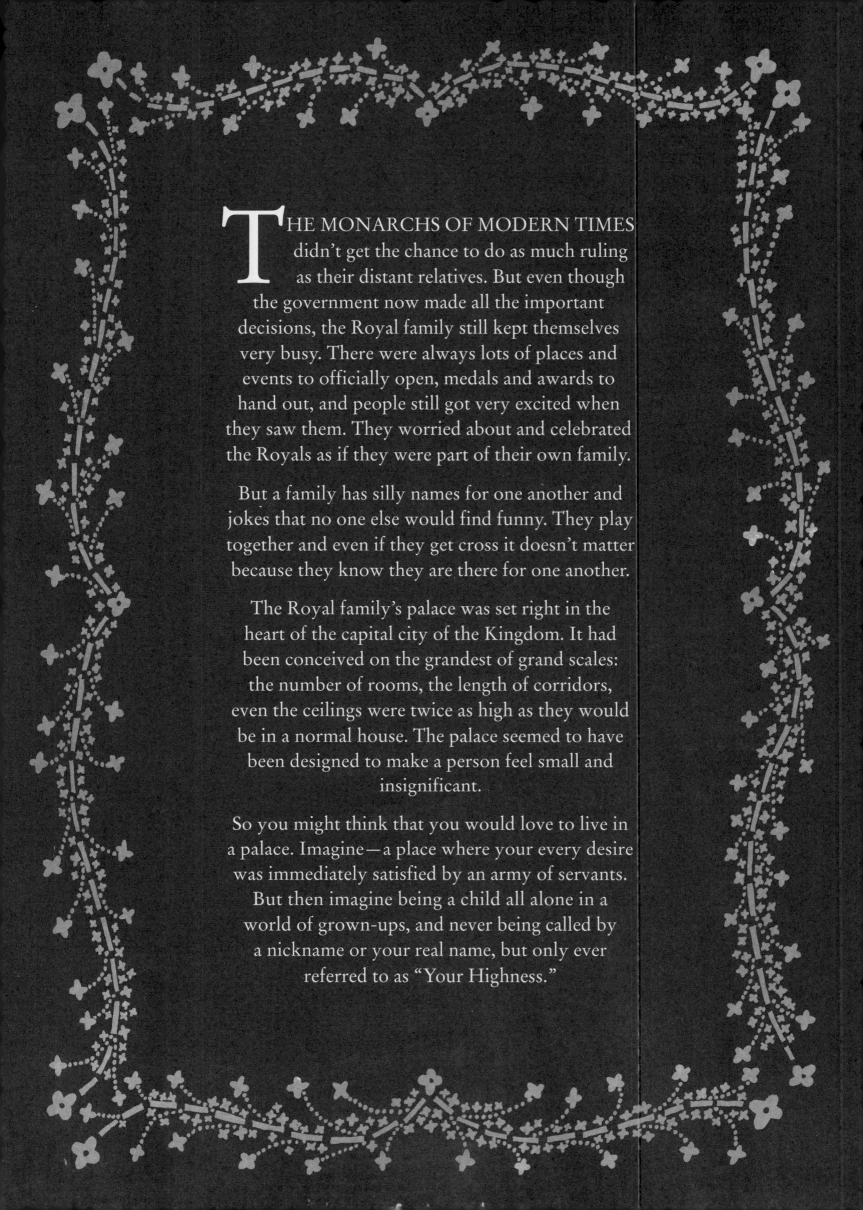

THE MONARCHS OF MODERN TIMES didn't get the chance to do as much ruling as their distant relatives. But even though the government now made all the important decisions, the Royal family still kept themselves very busy. There were always lots of places and events to officially open, medals and awards to hand out, and people still got very excited when they saw them. They worried about and celebrated the Royals as if they were part of their own family.

But a family has silly names for one another and jokes that no one else would find funny. They play together and even if they get cross it doesn't matter because they know they are there for one another.

The Royal family's palace was set right in the heart of the capital city of the Kingdom. It had been conceived on the grandest of grand scales: the number of rooms, the length of corridors, even the ceilings were twice as high as they would be in a normal house. The palace seemed to have been designed to make a person feel small and insignificant.

So you might think that you would love to live in a palace. Imagine—a place where your every desire was immediately satisfied by an army of servants. But then imagine being a child all alone in a world of grown-ups, and never being called by a nickname or your real name, but only ever referred to as "Your Highness."

THIS IS A STORY about a child like that: the King and Queen's only son.

Although the Prince's lonely situation seems sad to me, it didn't really seem sad to him. After all, he had never known any other kind of life.

He never left the palace to travel to school to run and play and sing and learn with other boys and girls; all his lessons were given to him by his own personal teacher in his own lonely classroom that contained just one desk.

The life of Lord Von Dronus, his tutor, was entirely devoted to serving the Royal family. His one and only purpose was to educate the Prince, a duty he undertook with immense seriousness. He was never friendly or kind to his solitary pupil for the simple reason that he had never been instructed to be. He lived his life according to rules, and he believed that they were to be obeyed to the last letter. Lord Von Dronus was in charge of teaching the Prince all the lessons any normal child would be taught, but also schooled this shy young boy in all the skills he would need for when he became King.

One of the questions that adults like asking children is, "What do you want to be when you grow up?" And a child can say anything—probable or improbable, ordinary or extraordinary. But no one ever asked the Prince who he'd like to be or what he dreamed of doing.

Everyone knew he was going to be one thing and one thing only—the King. His destiny was to reign, a job he would take over the day his father died.

The Prince attended to his lessons earnestly, no matter how strange or unusual they seemed. Was he happy or sad? It was hard to tell. He never really smiled, but then he never really frowned. He never complained about anything.

In fact, he was always so busy being lectured to that he never had much chance to speak at all.

ANOTHER THING THAT was different about the Prince was that he didn't spend a lot of time with his parents. The King and Queen didn't cook breakfast or dinner for him, or dry him roughly in front of the fire after he'd had his evening bath, or read him a story when it was bedtime; all of these things were done by the palace servants.

The young Prince very rarely saw his father. Hardly anyone ever saw the King. He was the shyest, most reclusive monarch who had ever reigned. He only appeared in public a few times a year, and then very reluctantly and only after much persuading by his ministers. He spent most of his time alone in his library.

It had once been a ballroom but now was filled with hundreds of shelves containing thousands of books that reached all the way up to the ceiling.

He took all his meals in the library seated at a long table. He spent every day in there writing, though nobody ever saw what he wrote.

As the King was so very elusive, the Queen's schedule was twice as busy. Her day was filled with meetings and speeches and talking to her loyal subjects —though she rarely spoke to her most loyal subject of all, her son.

FROM TIME TO TIME the Queen called on the Prince to attend an official engagement with her. Usually this meant some standing, followed by some bowing, and rounded off with some smiling. But on one occasion they left the palace to visit another part of the Kingdom.

The Royal family had their own train that they and their retinue traveled on. Far down below the deepest cellars and basements of the palace there was a single platform with a single train waiting at it with only one carriage. It was painted plain black and had dark tinted windows. The train went down a secret tunnel before it joined up with the other train lines. It was through these windows that the Prince saw his very first glimpse of the world outside the palace walls.

What he saw was nothing that you or I would find particularly fascinating, just a view of the backs of hundreds of little houses as the train passed through the city, gardens filled with laundry drying on clothes lines and sad, abandoned toys. But to the Prince, it was like watching a film that proved the existence of an entire civilization from a world that he had only previously heard rumors about. He wanted to know what was happening behind every window. He felt that it would take a hundred lifetimes to even begin to understand everything that went on outside the palace walls.

As the train moved slowly through the rain it came to a brief stop, and there, at one of the many windows, stood a small girl, about his age, looking out. The boy stared at her for all of the short time that the train waited there, although he knew she could not see him through the tinted glass. He watched her as she gazed out at the rain and, after all the many years of growing up an only child, he felt a deep longing to be her friend.

THE PALACE WORKED like a huge machine, not run by cogs and wheels but by courtiers and servants, where every person had their place and position. They knew the people above them who they should look up to and treat with respect, and they knew those below them who they could look down on and order around.

At the very bottom of the palace pecking order were the servants who had no one beneath them to boss around, such as the scullery maids and the pot scrubbers.

There was even a servant who sat alone all day in a basement surrounded by boots and shoes.

It was his job to clean and polish them all. He was the Bootman.

ACTUALLY, HE WAS NOT ALWAYS ALONE. Occasionally he had a visitor.

On one of his lonely wanderings around the palace, the young Prince found his way down to the Bootman's basement. Every servant in the palace treated the Prince with great formality. But here, in the dark and the damp, he finally found a warmer welcome.

Still only a young man himself, the Bootman was the only person in the palace who felt sorry for the boy and, although he occupied one of the lowest positions, he spoke to the Prince not as the future King but as a fellow person and, eventually, as a friend.

In turn, the young Prince was fascinated by the Bootman, entranced by the tiniest details of his life outside the palace. The Prince wanted to know what color his front door was painted, whether he preferred to sit upstairs or downstairs on the bus, what he did on his day off, what he ate for breakfast, and so on and so on . . .

Such relentless questioning might have driven anyone else crazy, but the Bootman didn't show any signs of impatience. He listened carefully as he carried on with his polishing and answered every question thoughtfully and honestly.

One day the young Prince asked the Bootman how he managed to remember who all the hundreds of shoes and boots that came in and out of the basement belonged to. The Bootman told the Prince that he could see the character of the owner in every crease and scruff on every boot and shoe.

"I have never given anyone back the wrong pair of boots," said the Bootman with considerable pride. "I had to devise a special way of knowing which boot belongs to which foot."

The Prince looked at the rows and rows of pointed toes and high heels. The boots with buttons and laces and zips. He thought of all the people who worked in the palace and all the different occasions that required a particular color of shoe or a certain type of boot. He couldn't imagine how the Bootman kept his kingdom in order.

"Would you like to be the only person in the world to know the secret besides me?" The young boy said "yes," so quietly it was almost a whisper.

The Bootman turned off the light switch and the room became pitch black.

Lord Braintree
Cherry Brown
PULL POLISH!

Lord Braintree Cherry Brown pull polish

Colonel Z.
Very Dark Brown
High Gloss.

Colonel Z. Very Dark Brow

* Colonel Z.
High Gloss

Lady Augusta
Ruby Red
Polish
(Fussy!)

Lady Augusta
Ruby Red
Polish
(Fussy!)

Major Briggs
Matt BLACK   NO SHINE!

Major Briggs
Matt BLACK   NO SHINE!!

Ma Brow

Mister
Ingrey
Plain
Chestnut

Mister
Ingre

Count Strunkel
Waterproof Plain
DUBBIN! Brown

Count Strunkel
Plain Brown
Waterproof Dubbin!

Very Shiny!
Sir Bourguin
Ebony Black

Sir Bourguin
Ebony Black!!!
Very Shiny!!!

Sir Ione
BLA

Lord Duggan
of Chelmsk Brown

Lord Three Coats
of Chestnut Brown

Lord Three
3 Coats Chestnut Brown

Master Peter
Plain
Black Polish

Master Peter

Plain
BLACK
Polish

Lady Harris
Special Polish
Purple Polish

Lady Harris
Special Polish
Purple Polish

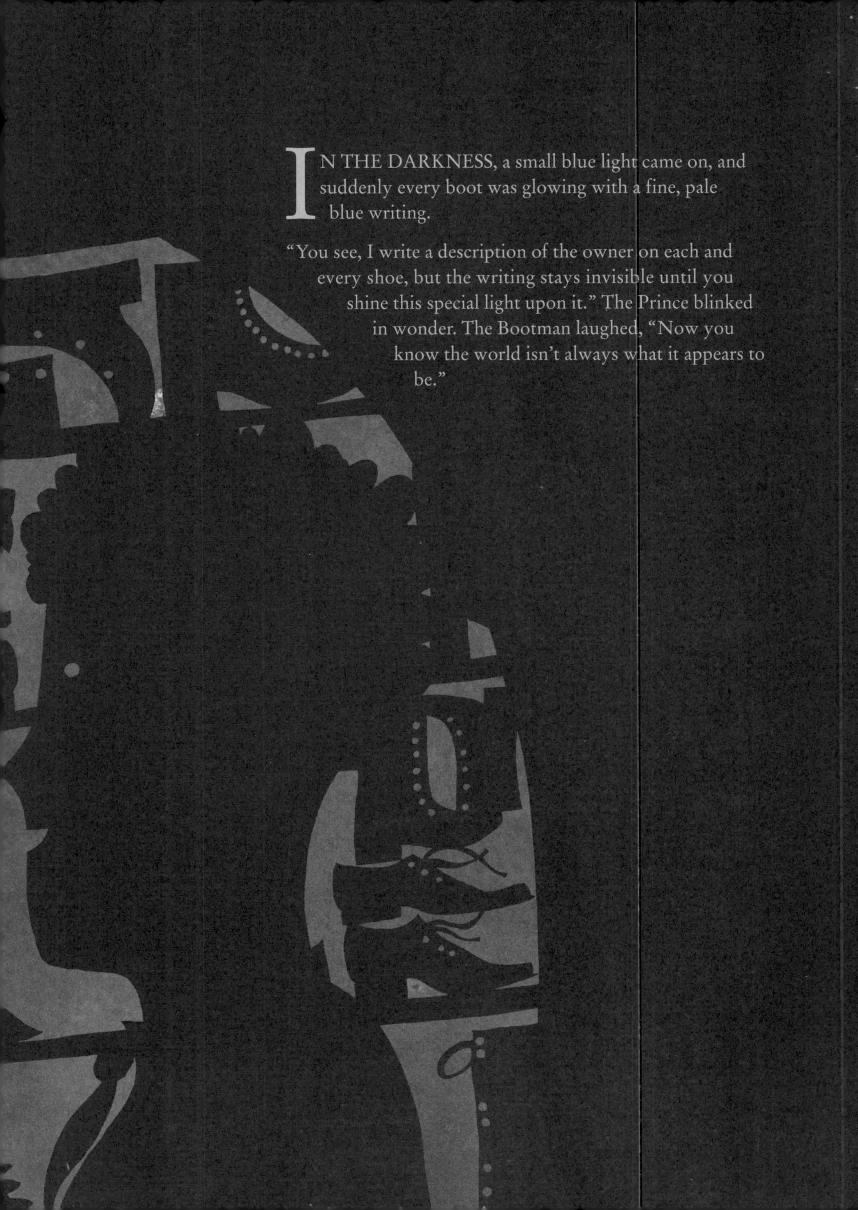

IN THE DARKNESS, a small blue light came on, and suddenly every boot was glowing with a fine, pale blue writing.

"You see, I write a description of the owner on each and every shoe, but the writing stays invisible until you shine this special light upon it." The Prince blinked in wonder. The Bootman laughed, "Now you know the world isn't always what it appears to be."

AS THE YOUNG PRINCE grew older, his timetable of lessons grew busier. Every minute of every day was filled with his training to become King. His meals became a lesson in correct table manners; walking down a corridor became a lesson in deportment. The only time the Prince really had to himself was when, at the end of another long day, he said goodnight to the bodyguard who kept watch outside his bedroom door and climbed into bed.

All day long this was the moment he looked forward to. That hour between getting into bed and falling asleep was the only time he could call his own, and every night he would lie still and return in his thoughts to an imaginary place of his own invention.

I T WAS A SMALL VILLAGE—a few streets and houses surrounded by fields, which in turn were surrounded by rolling hills. Returning there night after night, the Prince had populated this place with a cast of characters.

He had made up whole families, decided where they lived, worked, and shopped, and even what they ate for supper.

Cocooned inside the curtained walls of his grand four-poster bed, he would pretend he was taking a stroll down the main street of the little world he had created. As he walked along he called out "hello" to all the people he passed, and they all turned to him and smiled and said "hello" back.

ONE DAY, THE PRINCE had a wonderful idea and asked the Bootman if he could borrow one of the pens that wrote the invisible letters and also one of the special lights that revealed the pen's secret markings. The Bootman went to his stock cupboard and handed them to him.

"But don't you want to ask me what they're for?"

"No," said the Bootman.

"Even if it's for something really secret?" asked the Prince.

"Especially if it's for something really secret."

"But you told me the secret of the boots."

The Bootman replied, "I know that people need something to call their own. Even a king who can, at the click of his fingers, command anything he wants, any time he wants it, needs to have something that truly belongs to him alone, even if it is only a dream."

THAT NIGHT, with the special pen, the boy began to draw the village from his imagination all over the curtains that draped around his four-poster bed. Every night from then on, before he settled down to sleep, he would carry on with his work—drawing a house or extending part of a street—and then, when he was tired, he would get under his sheets and, using the special light, he would look at the world he had created.

As WEEKS AND months passed, the pictures on the curtains slowly grew and grew.

One night, after a satisfying hour of drawing, the young Prince was admiring his handiwork when he noticed that a small section of the curtain that covered the top of the bed had slightly come apart. Through this gap he could make out what looked like a small door handle.

With the help of a few pieces of precariously balanced furniture, the young Prince climbed up to investigate. It really was a handle, and when he turned it and pushed upwards, a small door opened.

AS THE PRINCE STRETCHED up to look inside, everything at first appeared to be pitch black. But as his eyes slowly got used to the darkness, he could see that he had found a room, quite tall and wide, and very long.

He had accidentally discovered the long-forgotten attic room.

In the past, the attic had been used as a handy dumping ground for things that were no longer needed, things such as bicycles that young princes and princesses had long since grown too big for, and unwanted statues of distant relatives nobody had ever really liked in the first place. As the years went by, the entrances that led into the attic had, one by one, been closed, sealed up, plastered and painted over.

Gradually, people forgot that the attic room even existed. In all the stories Lord Von Dronus had told the Prince about the history of the palace, in all he'd learned about its architecture and artifacts, no one had ever mentioned this magical space that ran uninterrupted all the way around, under the eaves.

With a glow of pure pleasure the young Prince realized that up here, right in the very heart of the palace where his every waking moment was scheduled and monitored, here in the dust and the dirt and the dark was a place he could truly call his own.

As he tentatively groped his way through the darkness, he decided he would make a map and work out exactly which room lay directly beneath each part of the attic.

BESIDES HIS NOCTURNAL adventures in the attic, the young Prince's busy routine went on as usual. However, as time passed by, the mood in the palace began to change.

When the King married the Queen he was significantly older than her, and when their only son, the Prince, was born many years later he was already an old man. Now, sadly, he was not only old but also very ill.

Although the palace had always been formal, it had also been busy and full of life, but now the sad news of the King's ill health spread from courtier to servant and it became a somber place; lights were dimmed, curtains were drawn, and voices were hushed.

One afternoon, the Prince was summoned to see his mother. In the presence of the Queen and her advisers he was officially reminded of the importance of "loyalty and tradition," as well as "his duty" and his "lonely destiny." The Prince understood the real meaning of this lecture.

It meant his father was dying.

Never before had the young Prince felt so empty and alone. As he walked away from the Queen's office, the palace, with all its grand splendor and beauty, had not one kind word of comfort to offer him.

H E CRIED TO HIMSELF until he found that his feet and his tears had carried him down to the basement room that belonged to his friend, the Bootman.

"My father is going to die and I don't want him to," he blurted out as he burst into tears and heaving sobs.

The Bootman put down his brush and did something that no one in the whole of the Prince's life had ever done before: he gathered up this poor, lonely boy and held him gently in his arms. When the boy had finally stopped sobbing and shaking the Bootman took out his handkerchief and wiped away all of the Prince's tears. Only then did he speak.

"Have you ever been on a roller coaster?"

The boy shook his head.

"The build-up as you slowly climb to the first peak is incredible; nothing has really happened yet, but the anticipation is so immense. When you make it to the top and then you plunge into free fall, you can hardly think straight because everything is going by so quickly. The sensations are so breathtaking, you can't take it all in. All you can do is scream! The second lap you can really start to enjoy the ride; you know what's coming and you're ready for it. On the third lap you can sit back and relax and just marvel at the wonderful views. By the final lap you're looking forward to the end. It has been incredible, but you've had enough now and you want to get off."

The Bootman smiled as he looked at the boy's perplexed face.

"And that's what life's like. It's this unbelievable ride, but you only get to ride it once. Your ride has barely even started and your father's ride is nearly over."

"But what if you don't like the ride you're on? What then?"
the young Prince asked.

THE KING'S HEALTH continued to deteriorate. Every day the young Prince asked Lord Von Dronus if he could visit his father, but every time he was put off with yet another excuse or told "perhaps tomorrow."

The Prince came to realize that he had never really known his father. His royal duties, his studying and writing had taken up all the time they could have spent together, and now time was running out for the young Prince to ask him all the questions that lay unanswered in his head, such as: "What were you like as a boy?"; "What have you been writing alone in your library all these years?"; "What do you think of me, if you ever think of me?"; "How can I be a good king?"

And although the frustration of being so young and powerless and always at the mercy of adults' decisions sometimes felt like it might consume him, one small thing saved his heart and mind from breaking apart.

Every single night throughout his father's long and final illness, the young Prince climbed up into the secret attic room and, using the diagram of the palace that he had mapped out, found the spot up there in the dark that was directly above the room where his father lay. Although he could neither see nor hear him, he felt comfort in knowing that he was as close to his father as he could be.

The Prince would bring a blanket and his light and he would sit up there all night, whispering down through the floorboards to the room below, "You are not alone, I am with you."

THE DAY FINALLY arrived when the Prince was summoned to see his dying father. As he entered the King's study, the thought struck him that this would be the first time that they had ever been alone together.

A small bed had been moved into the library, and as the Prince approached it he saw not a mighty king, powerful and imposing, but a weak and frail old man who was gradually fading away from life.

His skin was as dry as the parchment of the manuscripts that surrounded him, and the young boy felt that if he dared to touch him even ever so lightly, the King would crumble to dust.

As the young Prince knelt down beside him, the King tried to speak, but all that came out were wheezing gasps. This scholarly, bookish man, who throughout his life had surrounded himself with millions of words, now didn't even have one he could share.

The ailing monarch, with such great effort for so small a task, pulled out from beneath his bedcovers a large, ancient-looking key and, trembling, pressed it into his son's small hands.

Just at that moment, the royal physician came into the room. The boy quickly hid the mysterious key in his pocket as the King fell back onto his pillow.

The physician came over to the bed and listened to the King's heart beating faintly, then he turned to the young boy.

"It is late, let him rest now."

The young Prince kissed his father gently and quietly walked from the room.

When he got back to his own room he took the key from his pocket and examined it. It was quite rusty but he could read these words engraved along its shaft: *"My child, do not fear. I will always be here."*

THAT NIGHT, HE CLIMBED up into the attic once again to continue his vigil in the dark space directly above the room where his father lay sleeping.

As he sat there under his blanket, the young Prince started to cry until his tears overtook him and he couldn't stop, not even if he wanted to. At first came tears for his father and the thought of him dying, then came tears of self-pity because he had never really known his father as he imagined other children did, and then more tears because it was unfair that he had never had the chance to be like other children.

Tears because he realized that soon his father would die and he would have to be King himself, a person he never felt he was or ever could be. So many different types of tears. And when he realized he wasn't crying for his dying father but really he was crying for himself, he cried even more at his own wretched selfishness until he was utterly exhausted and sleep overwhelmed him.

But that same night, the saddest of his life, as he lay up there in the dark, unsure if he was awake or still in a dream, he saw a faint light hovering in the middle of the room like a twinkling star shining from a million miles away.

The young Prince stumbled up from the floor to investigate this strange, hovering apparition. And as he stood directly in front of it, close enough to reach out and touch it, he realized that it wasn't a star at all, but a tiny window no bigger than the smallest button on the cuff of a shirt. Leaning forward and peering through it he saw leaves and branches, and beyond them he could see the rooftops and towers of a great city sleeping in the cold light of early morning.

Taking his light from his pocket, the young Prince saw that the tiny window was actually just a hole in the middle of a window that had been covered with layer upon layer of thick black paint. Seeing a small clasp on the window's frame, he unfastened it and tried to pull the window up. It wouldn't budge. The paint that had been plastered all over the window had set it shut tight. He tried again, harder this time and with all the strength he had. For a brief moment he felt it shift ever so slightly. He tried once more, the paint cracked and parted and the window flew up and open!

The dull glow of early dawn flooded into the room, the first time in over a hundred years that fresh spring air, and light that had traveled all the way from its home on the sun, had reached that dark, forgotten place.

The leaves of a tall plane tree pushed against the palace wall as the boy peered out.

The feeling of incredible excitement at this momentous discovery was soon overtaken by one of panic as the young Prince realized that if it was morning then he was in danger of his absence from bed being discovered. Quickly closing the window, he rushed back to his bedroom as fast as he possibly could.

THE NEXT DAY BROUGHT SAD NEWS.

During the night, the old King had died. The hush that descended on the palace throughout his final days was now replaced by bustling activity as preparations were made for the funeral.

The great outpouring of grief at the King's death that swept across the whole country took the young Prince by surprise.

How can you mourn for someone who you never even knew? And he understood that he was thinking not of the King's grieving subjects but of himself.

The crowds that gathered on the day of the funeral were immense. Every street around the palace was packed with so many people that the funeral cortège could not even begin to make its way through them.

An improvised gangplank had to be raised above the crowds, balanced on the spears of the palace guards, so that the coffin could be carried over them.

As the body of their King passed above them, the people gasped in pity at the solitary figure walking behind the coffin with his head bowed.

How brave! How noble! How tragic! the crowd thought.

Seeing the swords and guns and uniforms of war all around him, the young Prince remembered the gentle old man who had loved books and words and peace, and he thought to himself how much his father would have hated all this.

As he marched slowly behind his father, he clutched the old rusty key in his hand and chanted under his breath, "My child, do not fear. I will always be here."

As THE ONLY CHILD in the entire palace,
the young Prince had never felt as if he really
belonged or fitted in anywhere.

But now he had become very much the center of attention.

Though the government decided that his mother, the Queen, would carry
out his royal duties until he turned eighteen, the day after the funeral,
the Prince was crowned King. He was thirteen.

As he sat on the throne, his feet a long way from the floor, through hours
of ceremonies filled with proclamations and declarations, it looked as
though he was solemnly taking it all in, but really he was thinking about
the window in the attic and everything that lay beyond it.

EVERY DAY SINCE his father's death, the young King's mind had been filled with thoughts of escaping from the palace through the secret attic window.

Every single night, he went up through the trapdoor above his bed to go and look out over the city. He felt the cool air blow across his face, enticing him, inviting him and daring him to leave the palace.

Finally, one night he climbed up into the attic not wearing his pajamas, but a dark hooded sweatshirt, dark trousers, and dark running shoes instead.

He opened the window as wide as it would go and stepped out onto its ledge.

He stopped for a moment, and as if he were addressing the whole city, or perhaps the entire country, he declared:

"All of my life I have lived according to the needs and demands of others. As far as they are concerned, I had but one destiny—that moment when they placed the crown on my head and claimed me as their personal property forever. But they are wrong. The moment of my destiny is now. This is my coronation, this is my crowning."

And as he launched himself into the night and flew through the air with his arms outstretched, he shouted, "God save the King!"

TWIGS AND LEAVES crashed into his face until he found himself clutching tightly onto a thick branch. Out of breath and trembling, the young King slowly climbed down through the branches, before dropping gently onto the soft grass.

Hiding behind a tree, he waited and watched in silence, not moving a muscle until he was absolutely sure that there was not a soul about, then he darted to the next tree and again looked anxiously around. He repeated this over and over again, until at last he came to some railings. He climbed over them and dropped down. He was on the sidewalk.

NOW THAT HE WAS finally outside the palace, the young King felt unsure what to do or where to go, but as he began to walk down the silent streets he made a map in his head of where he had been, just in case he got lost. After all, the King, especially one in disguise, could hardly ask someone for directions to the palace.

As he wandered through the city, he walked past strange bundled-up shapes lying on park benches and in shop doorways, then realized that they were people.

IN OTHER DOORWAYS he saw lovers who held each other in their arms and whispered secret promises.

He saw people out walking dogs and he saw people sitting alone in an all-night café. Down one street he passed a noisily humming building which spat out bundles of newspapers from a chute in its side onto the street where men waited to load them into vans to deliver them to newsstands across the city.

He passed countless statues and churches and heard the bells in their clock towers striking on the hour, though hardly anyone else was awake to hear them. He saw traffic lights constantly changing, with no cars to obey them.

Seeing a light glowing in a basement window, he crossed the street to take a closer look. In the steamy warmth of their kitchen, bakers were rolling out the dough for the bread that would be eaten all over the city the following morning. As he listened to them chatting and joking to one another as they worked, the delicious aroma of bread baking rose up and he breathed it in greedily. It was the most beautiful thing he had ever smelled.

WHEN HE CAME to the river, he climbed up onto its embankment wall and looked all around. He saw not a single soul anywhere, but he didn't feel lonely at all.

Holding onto a lamp post, he lifted his head towards the night sky and sang:

"As traffic lights change unwatched,

And bells ring each hour unheard,

I walk the streets alone as slowly as

The world turns, just like a ghost.

Nobody sees me and no one hears me,

Nobody even knows I'm here at all.

This night, this moment is what I've longed

For all of my life.

And if I were truly a king I'd command Time

To stop! Right now!

And live here in this moment for ever."

AS HE SANG TO HIMSELF, the young King glanced across to the east and saw the sky was getting brighter. Dawn was coming. Reluctantly, he began to retrace his steps—past the bakery, past the churches, past the all-night café— all the way to the palace. He climbed over the railings and back up the tree to the attic window. Then he ran back to his room where his unslept-in bed lay waiting.

The next day the young King couldn't concentrate on his lessons at all. Even though his body was exhausted from hardly having any sleep, his mind was wide awake.

He felt he would explode if he didn't share his amazing discovery with someone. After his lessons he made his way to the basement.

"I have an incredible secret that I have to share with you—" he began, but the Bootman swiftly cut him short.

"Don't say another word! The greatest secret in the world is the secret that is never told. At first it seems so big that you feel as if you can't hold it in, but if you manage to keep it within yourself you will see it begin to grow into something more rich and more beautiful than you ever could have imagined."

AND SO THE YOUNG King's nighttime excursions remained private. Although his journeys never had any particular destination, they were not completely without purpose. In his pocket he always carried the old key that his father gave to him on his deathbed. Deep down inside he felt that the words engraved along its length held a message that was meant just for him, and everywhere he went he was always looking for some kind of sign or clue to its meaning.

IN SOME QUIET PARTS of the city, the young King could walk for miles without seeing a single person.

So it was a joy when he came across the wholesale fish market, lit up not just with blazing lamps but with shouts and laughter as the busy porters hauled huge boxes of the day's catch into trucks to go to fish and chip shops to be battered and fried and eaten with salt and vinegar and pleasure.

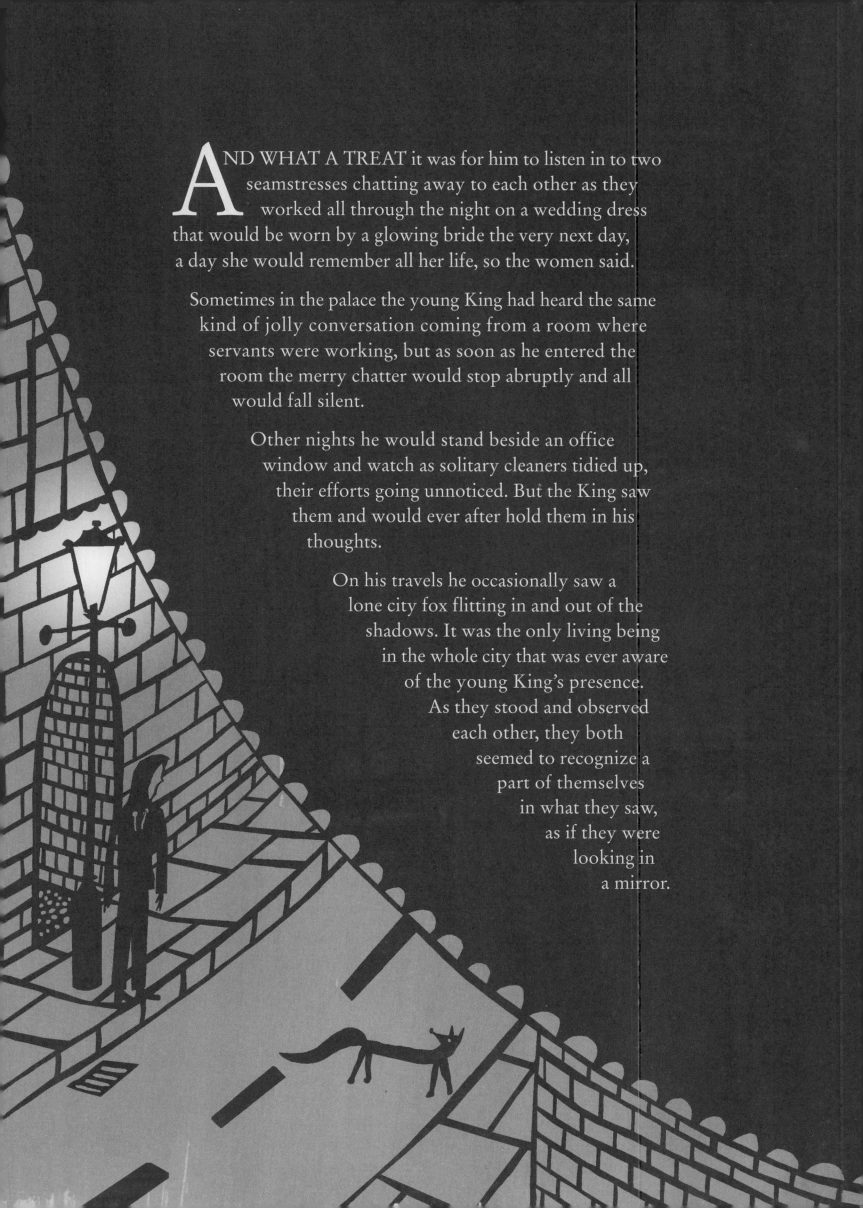

AND WHAT A TREAT it was for him to listen in to two seamstresses chatting away to each other as they worked all through the night on a wedding dress that would be worn by a glowing bride the very next day, a day she would remember all her life, so the women said.

Sometimes in the palace the young King had heard the same kind of jolly conversation coming from a room where servants were working, but as soon as he entered the room the merry chatter would stop abruptly and all would fall silent.

Other nights he would stand beside an office window and watch as solitary cleaners tidied up, their efforts going unnoticed. But the King saw them and would ever after hold them in his thoughts.

On his travels he occasionally saw a lone city fox flitting in and out of the shadows. It was the only living being in the whole city that was ever aware of the young King's presence. As they stood and observed each other, they both seemed to recognize a part of themselves in what they saw, as if they were looking in a mirror.

AFTER THIS ENCOUNTER, the young King climbed up the ladder of a towering crane and sang:

"Now, at last, I know who I am.

I'm the secret brother of the city fox!

I shouldn't really even be here,

But I am, slipping in and out of the shadows,

Always hiding but never seen.

Like a fox, I am always looking

But I don't know quite what for.

The people nobody thinks about, that's whose side I'm on.

I'll hold onto this feeling

All of my life and recall it when I'm King, and I'll rule

Not just with my mind but also with my heart."

AS THE YEARS passed by, the King grew from being a young boy to almost a grown man.

Every encounter he had with the real world diminished his interest in the artificial world of the palace, and Lord Von Dronus grew increasingly suspicious of the King's unaccountable exhaustion during his lessons.

Then one day, a few months short of his eighteenth birthday, he was summoned once more to a meeting with the Queen's ministers, and as he made his way along the palace corridors he felt somehow that bad news was on its way.

HE WAS RIGHT. The council of ministers read to him a proclamation ordering him to vacate his bedroom the following morning.

Now his official duties were due to begin, he would have to be moved to the King's apartments to be protected by more bodyguards, and to accommodate a much larger retinue of valets and footmen as befitted his status.

Even though he knew that this announcement had been coming, he felt his legs wobble beneath him as if he were a prisoner, who had just been handed a life sentence by a judge. Which in a way he had.

Leaving behind his bedroom meant losing access to his trapdoor, the only way into the attic, which meant bringing an end to his nightly adventures outside the palace.

As he left the meeting, the young King was utterly distraught.

He made his way down to the basement to see the only person to whom he could say out loud the thoughts he held in his head.

"I don't want to be King. I can't be King," he cried out in despair. And the Bootman did the kindest thing any person can do for another: he listened.

As the young King spoke of his doubts and fears, the Bootman sat and nodded until eventually it seemed as if the King had run out of words and fell silent.

"We all have to do things that we don't want to in life, we just have to make the best of it," the Bootman said. "Life is what you make it, it's up to you. It's all in your hands."

"BUT MY LIFE has never been in my hands," the young King replied.

"Well, be that as it may, none of us knows what the future holds," the Bootman said as he poured a large, steaming mug of tea for the young man. "We just have to do our best."

As he walked back to his room, the young King resolved to go out one last night to say goodbye to this other world. As he climbed out the window and down through the branches of the tree, he remembered the Bootman's words and felt consoled.

The Bootman is right, he thought to himself, *none of us really knows what the future holds.*

To his amazement, the city that night was not the sleepy, peaceful place he was used to. A fantastic carnival filled the streets with thousands of people singing and dancing.

The young King couldn't help but be swept along with the current of the crowd. He had never been among so many people before and the mood was intoxicating.

At the same time, though, he was nervous that someone might recognize him. Whenever he had escaped from the palace before, he had avoided any kind of contact with other people, and now here he was dancing along with a vast crowd!

BECOMING AWARE of the danger of his situation, he spotted a narrow side street leading off the main road and managed to break away from the revelers.

As he walked further along this street he had not been down before, he saw a huge key hanging up high on the wall above him. As he got nearer, he began to make out in the half-light the words painted on a plaque hanging beneath it.

His heart jumped into his mouth as he read the inscription: "My child, do not fear. I will always be here."

He reached into his trouser pocket and retrieved the key he always carried with him.

Beneath the sign was an old metal gate to a narrow alley from which came a dull red glow.

H
E INSERTED THE KEY into the lock. It was a perfect fit.

The young King's hands were shaking with excitement as he began to turn the old key in its long-lost home. The message his father meant for him would at last be delivered.

The lock clicked open. The King glanced down the street to check it was all clear, only to see a solitary figure walking along the pavement towards him!
As he stared at the approaching stranger, he recognized the silhouette. It was none other than Lord Von Dronus!

As quickly as he could, he snapped the lock shut, turned and hurried back down the street towards the teeming crowds.

The thought of his tutor spotting him filled the young King with horror and he broke out in a sickly, cold sweat as he rushed and pushed through the crowds as fast as his legs would carry him.

I N A BLIND PANIC, he had but one thought: to get back to the palace before his absence was discovered. He scrambled over the railings, ran across the grass, and clambered up the tree so quickly his hands were cut all over by its rough branches.

He rushed through the dark attic back to his bedroom and as soon as he had closed the trapdoor he got beneath his bedcovers still wearing his outdoor clothes.

In the corridor outside he heard heavy footsteps running and seconds later Lord Von Dronus and four palace guardsmen burst into his room.

"Don't you believe in knocking anymore?" said the young King as he pretended to yawn.

The look of pure fury on Lord Von Dronus's face left the King in no doubt that his secret had finally been uncovered. "We . . . we had reason to believe Your Majesty's life was in danger," the Lord stammered angrily.

"Well, obviously I'm perfectly well," the young King replied calmly, as if the entire conversation bored him utterly, although his heart was pounding. "Please would you close the door on your way out?"

With nothing more to say, the furious Lord departed with the guardsmen.

THE NEXT MORNING came and the young King was woken by a delegation of courtiers who had come to escort him to the King's official apartments. In a moment of sudden inspiration, the King declared he had a fever. It would be out of the question for him to move anywhere at all today.

"But it is for Your Highness's safety," protested Lord Von Dronus. He knew that somewhere in this room there must be a way out of the palace and as soon as he had the King removed, he was planning on tearing the room apart to find it.

Just at that moment, the Queen entered and the young King quickly began to tell her how he not only had a headache, but a stomachache and an earache as well.

The Queen looked fondly at the King, and although he was now almost a man, she still saw before her a small boy—her son.

In the steely voice the Queen reserved for when she did not intend to be questioned, she announced grandly, "I will nurse my son myself all today and tonight. He shall move in the morning." Of course, nobody, not even Lord Von Dronus, dared to challenge her.

That day, the King spent more time with his mother than he had in the last ten years put together. They chatted and laughed, told stories and sang songs they remembered from the days when he was a child.

It was a magical day. The happiest the young King could ever remember.

FINALLY EXHAUSTED, they both lay down to sleep.

The young King listened to his mother's breathing as it became heavier and she fell into a deep slumber. Only then, after briefly kissing her farewell, did he climb up to the trapdoor above his bed and into the attic room.

As he dropped down into the garden, he noticed at once that guardsmen had been posted on all the streets around the palace. It would have seemed that the palace was being especially vigilant about someone breaking in; however, the truth was really the other way around.

Luckily, the young King had over the years had lots of practice moving between the city's shadows, and he silently slipped past the guards unseen.

FILLED WITH APPREHENSION, he made his way through the city. He worried that at any moment his absence from the palace might be discovered. Keeping off the main roads, he cut down every dark alley and side street he knew, until finally he stood before the iron gate beneath the huge key.

He turned his cherished key in the lock and pushed the gate open. A narrow brick-lined corridor, like a short tunnel, led him to a small chamber.

In the chamber there was a statue of an old man kneeling down with his arms outstretched. In his hands he held a key. His face was kind. It seemed to the King that the statue knew exactly who he was and had been awaiting his arrival for a very long time.

Beneath the old man, these words were carved on his pedestal.

When I held you as
a baby in my arms,
I never imagined
you as you stand
here today.

And it seems like
only yesterday
when, with my
whole life before me,
I stood where you
stand now.

What would I say
to my younger self
that now I can only
say to you?

Could I give you a
key that would open
all the doors that lie
ahead of you?

The only real
wisdom I have
acquired in all these
long years is this
small pearl I now
place in your hands.

Do the things that you believe in your heart are true,
even though the whole world might disagree.

Prefer to be poor and free, rather than a slave to riches.
Smile willingly and help others if you can.
Be kind and honest and happy and true,
and every door in the city will open to you.

And when you feel completely alone, my child,
do not fear—for you know that
I will always be here.
Deep in your heart, your whole life through.

As he read these
words, he heard his
own father's voice
speaking to him,
and the emptiness
he had felt inside
gradually seemed to
fill up and up until
he felt not full, not
overflowing . . .
but complete.

WHAT THE YOUNG King didn't know, as he locked the gate behind him and walked out into the cool night air, was that the courtyard he had discovered wasn't really a secret at all.

The chamber and the statue with the inscription had been built centuries before by one of the founding fathers of the city. The man had married late in life, and when he fell ill and realized he would die before his son was grown up, he decided to create a place where, when his son was old enough, he would be able to share what life had taught him. He left instructions that the key to the gate should be passed down through the generations.

Though the key in the King's hand was the original, over the years, countless copies of this key had been made. A long, long time ago, no one knows exactly when, it was decided that every father should give their children a key when they turned eighteen. Every boy and girl would find their way to the courtyard, stand alone under the benign gaze of the old man, and read the inscription.

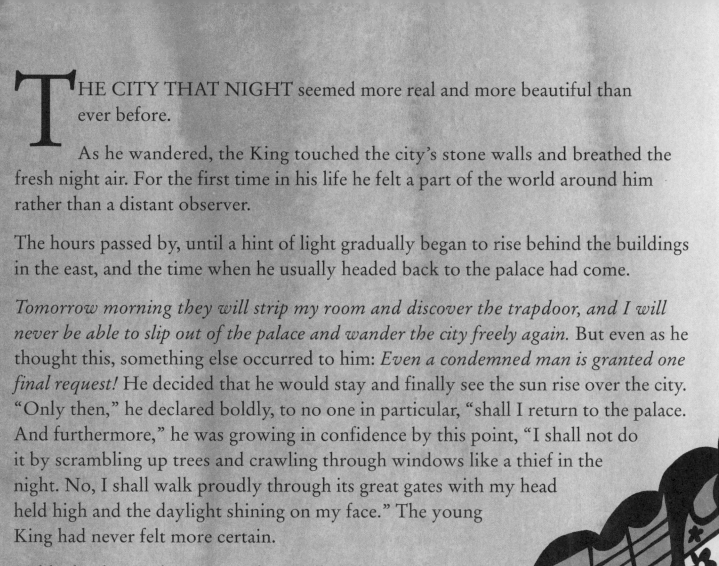

THE CITY THAT NIGHT seemed more real and more beautiful than
ever before.

As he wandered, the King touched the city's stone walls and breathed the
fresh night air. For the first time in his life he felt a part of the world around him
rather than a distant observer.

The hours passed by, until a hint of light gradually began to rise behind the buildings
in the east, and the time when he usually headed back to the palace had come.

*Tomorrow morning they will strip my room and discover the trapdoor, and I will
never be able to slip out of the palace and wander the city freely again.* But even as he
thought this, something else occurred to him: *Even a condemned man is granted one
final request!* He decided that he would stay and finally see the sun rise over the city.
"Only then," he declared boldly, to no one in particular, "shall I return to the palace.
And furthermore," he was growing in confidence by this point, "I shall not do
it by scrambling up trees and crawling through windows like a thief in the
night. No, I shall walk proudly through its great gates with my head
held high and the daylight shining on my face." The young
King had never felt more certain.

Suddenly, the city began to wake up all around
him. The first buses of the day came creeping
sleepily from their garages, and on
every street shopkeepers began
to raise the shutters on
their windows.

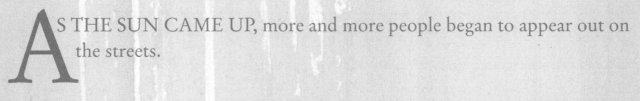

AS THE SUN CAME UP, more and more people began to appear out on the streets.

To everyone else, there wouldn't have been anything exceptional about this morning, but to the young King, it seemed like the most wonderful symphony you could ever hear! An opera! The greatest book you could ever read, but even better because in this incredible story unfolding before his eyes he could actually play a part and even change the course of the story itself!

With a clarity he'd never experienced before, the young King realized that all this was what he really wanted. This was what the inscription must have meant about being true to yourself. He wanted to be a part of this city, these streets, this world more than anything else. He wanted to tear off all his clothes and dive head first into this swirling sea of life.

He had always felt somehow out of place, as if he never really belonged anywhere. Not as a boy, not as a Prince and certainly not as a King. But right now, sitting here alone on this busy street, he had never felt more at home.

HE WALKED ALONG as if in a dream. Not thinking, not even looking where he was going, he wandered until he noticed that his feet had carried him back down the avenue that led straight to the palace.

Before him loomed the vast stone edifice of the Royal Palace in all its magnificent grandeur. A monument that thousands of sightseers traveled thousands of miles to stare at, awed by the history and tradition it represented.

BUT THE YOUNG King saw none of this. All he saw was a giant gravestone.

He stood up straight and held it in his gaze before he finally spoke, clearly and loudly, as if he were addressing a vast crowd.

"I'm never going back."

He turned around and, never once looking behind him, walked away from his family home, heading back into the bustling streets of the city.

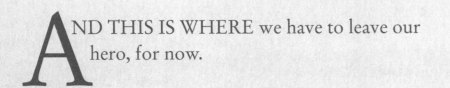

ND THIS IS WHERE we have to leave our hero, for now.

After all those years of searching, he had finally found his heart's desire and was determined to pursue it come what may.

But the city could be as harsh and uncaring as it was exciting and bewitching, and to be honest I'm worried for him. How would he survive without all of the things we have that we take for granted? No money, no home, no friends, no help! Just the clothes on his back.

We can only wait and see…

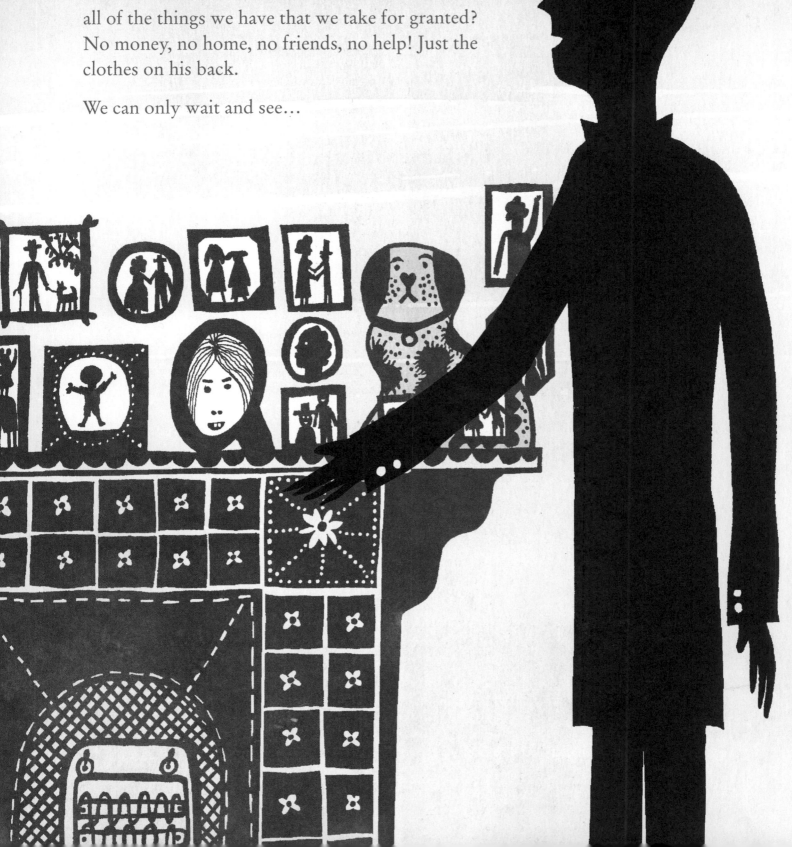

First American edition published in 2016 by
CROCODILE BOOKS
An imprint of Interlink Publishing Group, Inc.
46 Crosby Street, Northampton, Massachusetts 01060
www.interlinkbooks.com

Published in Great Britain by Hutchinson, Random House

Library of Congress Cataloging-in-Publication Data

Ryan, Rob, 1962-
The invisible kingdom / Rob Ryan.
pages cm
Summary: A lonely young prince finds a way to escape the palace and experience the real
world.
ISBN 978-1-56656-077-1
[1. Princes--Fiction. 2. Loneliness--Fiction. 3. Self-actualization (Psychology)--Fiction.] I.
Title.

PZ7.1.R95In 2015
[Fic]--dc23

2015025189

Text design by Carrdesignstudio.com

Printed and bound in Italy

Special thanks to Miss Liberty Wright who did all the hard work!